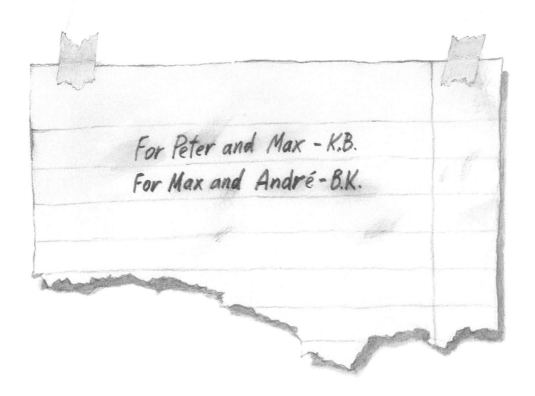

For Peter and Max – K.B.
For Max and André – B.K.

Text copyright © 2010 by Kate Banks
Pictures copyright © 2010 by Boris Kulikov
Distributed in Canada by D&M Publishers, Inc.
Color separations by Chroma Graphics PTE Ltd.
Printed in October 2009 in China by C&C Joint Printing Co.,
Shenzen, Guangdong Province
Designed by Robbin Gourley
First edition, 2010
10 9 8 7 6 5 4 3 2 1

www.fsgkidsbooks.com

Library of Congress Cataloging-in-Publication Data
Banks, Kate, date.
    The eraserheads / Kate Banks ; pictures by Boris Kulikov.— 1st ed.
        p. cm.
    Summary: Three eraserheads that live with a boy in the land of pencils, paper, rulers,
numbers, letters, and drawings become trapped in one of his pictures while trying to
correct mistakes.
    ISBN: 978-0-374-39920-7
    [1. Erasers—Fiction.   2. Drawing—Fiction.   3. Adventures and adventurers—
Fiction.]   I. Kulikov, Boris, ill.   II. Title.

PZ7.B22594 Erc 2010
[E]—dc22
                                                                                2008024144

The ERAZERHEADS

pictures by
Boris Kulikov

Kate Banks

FRANCES FOSTER BOOKS • Farrar, Straus and Giroux
New York

Once there were three eraserheads:
an owl, a crocodile, and a pig.
They lived with a boy in the land of pencils,
paper, rulers, letters, numbers, and drawings.
And they had an important job.
They erased mistakes.

"Over here," cried the crocodile, racing to the scene of a math problem.

4 + 3 = 8.

"Whoops! That's not right," said the crocodile.

The crocodile was good with numbers.

He erased the eight.

The boy put a seven in its place.

Sometimes the crocodile erased sloppy numbers.

Or numbers that were written upside down.

The owl was good with letters and words.
Often a letter was too large, or sometimes too small.
There were letters which appeared backward.
There were words where they didn't belong.
And they all needed erasing.

The pig liked to eat. He would erase
just about anything.
But he was shy and afraid of animals
larger than himself.

One day the eraserheads were sitting on the edge of
the boy's desk, watching a large picture take form.
There was a beach with buckets and shovels
and an umbrella.
Shells glittered in the sand.

The boy began to draw a road leading away from the beach.
"I wonder where it's going," said the pig.
"We'd better follow it," said the owl.
The road began to wind. It twisted and turned.
It passed a small house.
But suddenly the boy ran out of space.

So the crocodile began erasing the road.
He had intended to erase just a small section,
but he got carried away.
He rubbed and rubbed until he'd erased the road completely.
And the eraserheads were left in the middle of nowhere.

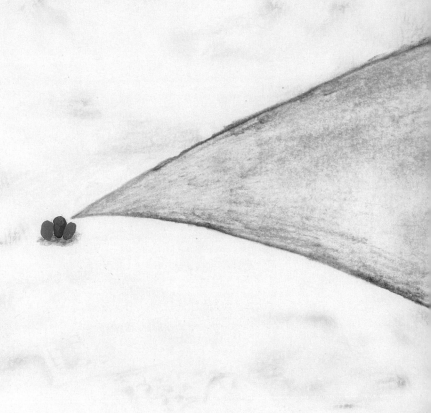

"Oops," said the crocodile. He blushed and his cheeks turned red.
"I've made a mistake. We're supposed to correct mistakes, not make them."
"It's okay," said the pig. "Everyone makes mistakes."
"It's a good thing," said the owl. "Or we wouldn't have any work."
"But what do we do now?" said the crocodile.

Then suddenly, from the middle of the paper,
a large wave came their way.
It swept up the eraserheads . . .

. . . and carried them off to a desert island.
The boy had drawn palm trees on the island, and a small hut.

Then he began to draw some wild animals.
He drew a monkey, and a snake.
"I'm not sure I like it here," said the pig.

The boy drew a tiger.
At first he gave it long pointed teeth.
But then he changed his mind.
"I can't erase those," said the pig. "I'm too scared."
"I'll do it," said the owl, and he went to work.
"My head is sore," he said when he'd finished.

The boy began to draw a bridge back to dry land.
But he made a mistake.

He didn't like what he'd drawn, so he picked up the
paper and crumpled it into a ball.
Then the boy got up and left the room.
And the eraserheads were stranded on a crumpled
island on a corner of the crumpled paper with some
very scary animals.
"What are we going to do?" said the pig.
He looked at the tiger and shivered.
He looked at the snake, who seemed to
be moving toward them.

Then the crocodile had an idea.
He began erasing the snake.
He erased a little bit here and a
little bit there.
Soon an SOS appeared on the crumpled paper,
which had begun to slowly unfurl.
When the boy returned, he saw the call for help.
He saw the eraserheads looking worn and dirty.

The boy smoothed out the paper and went back to
his drawing.
He drew a sign pointing to the beach.
Then he drew a boat and wrote his name on the stern.
Soon the eraserheads found themselves drifting
pleasantly across the sea.
"Hooray for mistakes," cried the owl.
"Yes," said the crocodile, who'd been imagining a world
with no mistakes.
"There'd be nothing to learn," he said.
The pig nodded. "And what fun would that be?"
Then he erased the crest of a large wave heading their way.
"Hooray for erasers," said the crocodile.

"Hooray for life preservers," said the pig,
who was caught by a wave.

Then, with the pig safe and sound, the eraserheads sailed home.